The Christmas Dragon

By Stanley Lombardo

Illustrations by Miranda Ponder

For my mother, Josephine Gullo Lombardo,
For my son, Lucas Sebastian,
And as always, for my Sun Woman

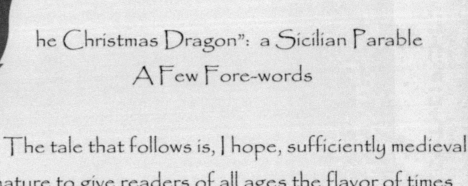

"The Christmas Dragon": a Sicilian Parable
A Few Fore-words

The tale that follows is, I hope, sufficiently medieval in nature to give readers of all ages the flavor of times long past and distant realms, without taxing the modern reader with too many archaic or obscure words. However, some old-fashioned and foreign words are necessary to set the tone for the story, as well as for the meter of the lines, though I have endeavored to keep the meter light and informal. For those readers who might be put off by the medieval-sounding vocabulary, to say nothing of the words I've preserved in Italian, I offer the following Quick-Reference Glossary before you encounter these terms in the tale of the Christmas Dragon.

Dragon, Serpent, Snake, Worm, Wyrm –
All of these terms can refer to a Dragon or reptile of any kind, and
I've applied them interchangeably to refer to the transformed Marquis.

Largess – Generosity, especially in the charitable
sense of giving liberally to those less privileged.

Marquis – A nobleman, originally the protector of lands
bordering a hostile kingdom. It is pronounced variously "Mar-kee,"
"Mar-kiss," "Mar-kwis," or in one long stretch "Mar-kwish" (to rhyme
with "wish"). Although medieval titles such as "Duke," "Earl," "Marquis,"
et al. originally had specific meanings, the distinctions gradually faded
until they were, in effect, interchangeable; hence, in the story, the
Marquis of Monte Maggiore is sometimes referred to as a Duke.

Noblesse – Nobility. It is probably best known from the
expression "Noblesse oblige" – "Nobility obligates."
(That is, the condition of being noble confers
obligations upon the nobleman or woman.)

Strega – Italian: witch

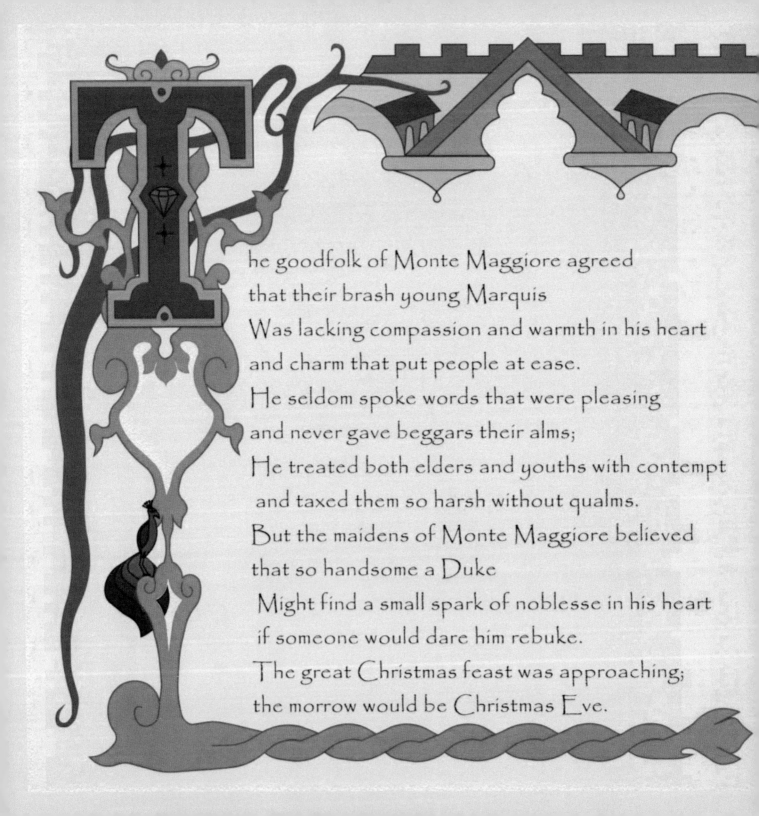

The goodfolk of Monte Maggiore agreed
that their brash young Marquis
Was lacking compassion and warmth in his heart
and charm that put people at ease.
He seldom spoke words that were pleasing
and never gave beggars their alms;
He treated both elders and youths with contempt
and taxed them so harsh without qualms.
But the maidens of Monte Maggiore believed
that so handsome a Duke
Might find a small spark of noblesse in his heart
if someone would dare him rebuke.
The great Christmas feast was approaching;
the morrow would be Christmas Eve.

All hoped that the magic of Yule might bring change and cause the Marquis to believe.
The strega they called La Befana, a woman both clever and wise,
Decided to tempt the young scoundrel to thaw and faced him that day in disguise.

She saw him at noon in the
market, selecting a shining new sword;
Concealed as an elderly beggar in rags, she spoke to him: "Most mighty Lord —
"I pray thee, most excellent Marquis, to succor me in my distress:

"I am the grandmother of seven
small tykes whom scarcely I may feed and dress."
"But what's that to me?" asked the Marquis. "Those urchins are none of my care.
"Your task is to feed them and clothe them yourself." Befana said, "Marquis, beware!

"I offer you hope of redemption –
a chance to choose Charity's way,
"But if you persist in your dragonish heart,
you'll turn wyrm by the end of the day."
The Marquis just laughed at the strega,
though he ought to have heeded her screed;
He thought to return to his dragonish hoard,
to revel in his selfish greed.
"Old woman, go back to your children;
your threats are as empty as air:
"You know I'm a nobleman out of your star."
"Defy me," she said, "if you dare."

"You've now had your chance," said Befana; "I hoped to entice you to change.

"A dragon you are, in your heart, greedy man, all kindness remains to you strange.

This geas that I now lay upon you condemns you to your proper form:
"A dragon you've been in your heart all your life, so I doom you to live as a worm!"

In view of the folk of the city, the wise woman conjured her spell:
The Marquis assumed a dread serpentine form, fore'er as a Dragon to dwell!

The Dragon-Duke stared at his body, aghast at each talon and scale:
His smooth skin had turned into dragonish hide, enhanced by a long, forkèd tail.

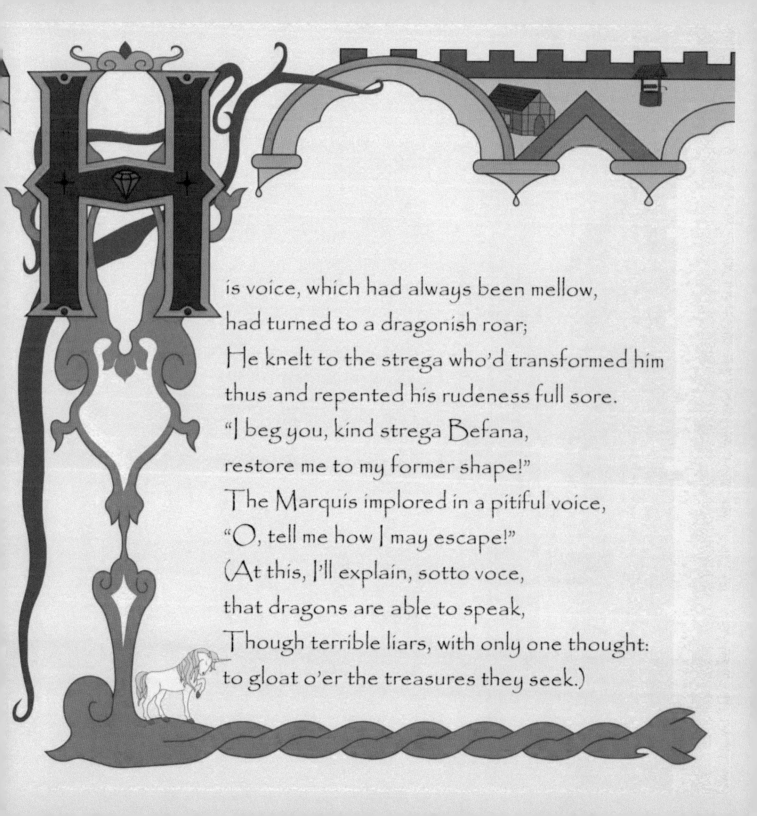

His voice, which had always been mellow,

had turned to a dragonish roar;

He knelt to the strega who'd transformed him

thus and repented his rudeness full sore.

"I beg you, kind strega Befana,

restore me to my former shape!"

The Marquis implored in a pitiful voice,

"O, tell me how I may escape!"

(At this, I'll explain, sotto voce,

that dragons are able to speak,

Though terrible liars, with only one thought:

to gloat o'er the treasures they seek.)

The Strega was not without pity, not even for this wretched Snake.
She wanted to teach him a lesson or six and his terrible arrogance shake.
"You've only one chance," said Befana, "and that I shall tell you anon.

"You must give away your most coveted things till all of your treasures are gone."

"But – all of my treasures?" he wheedled, a plaintive appeal in his voice.

"All right, then," she said, "just with seven dispense, but each must be your hardest choice:

"Distribute your wealth to the needy; consign seven gifts to the poor;

"So sacrifice all that your greed has held dear, and your human shape I'll restore."

"Bring all of your gifts to the fountain in Monte Maggior's marketplace;

"In public you must cast your hoardings away, or forever you'll live in disgrace."
The Marquis who now was a Dragon, quick summoned his Esquire to fetch
The most precious objects he held in his vaults, "And please do so quickly, thou wretch!"

And these were the treasures they witnessed,
the playthings of their spendthrift Lord:
A Warhorse, a Chalice, a Sword, and a Bow,
plus three more choice things from his hoard;
A great Silver Box filled with Relics
he'd gathered from shrines far and wide,
A Harp that produced most mellifluous notes,
and a Ruby Ring fit for a bride.
He laid out his treasures before him,
the seven things that he held dear,
And at this first sign of a softening heart,
the townsfolk gave out a great cheer.
The Sword he bestowed on the Esquire,
the son of his father's dear friend,

"I knight you and give you this trenchant
steel blade, that you may our fair homeland defend."
The blithe Esquire welcomed it gladly, he pressed his young lips to the blade.
"Sir Marquis, I thank you for this gracious gift -- while I wield it, no foe shall invade!"

His Charger he offered the Milkman, who needed a horse for his cart;
Without a good steed, he must pull it himself, which caused him to stumble and smart.
"Of what use to me is a warhorse?" the Milkman inquired with a shrug;

"He'd most likely charge down the street, as at war, and break every bottle and jug.

"I'd rather your gentle old ambler, the lowliest prized of your herd:

"She'll pull my old cart at a dignified pace that a warhorse would think quite absurd."

He offered the Grail to the Vintner,
who gratefully took it in hand,
But said, "My fine wines have no need for such show,
yet a chalice of glass would be grand."
The Dragon-Lord ordered his Esquire to bring them a goblet of glass.

As crystalline-clear as a crisp winter's night, worth many a farthing of brass.
"The Grail I'll bestow on the abbey," the Dragon-Duke then stoutly vowed,
"Where, daily, they celebrate God's holy Mass and offer up orisons loud."

The Harp that belonged to King David, he gave to a cherub-voiced Boy,
Whose songs so rejoiced whosoever did hear that even sad hearts swelled with joy.

His eyes shining great with this wonder,
the Boy-Bard accepted the Harp
And struck a melodious chord on its strings,
which rang out in the square clear and sharp.
And all of the townsfolk who heard it
experienced hearts filled with joy,
Spontaneously praising the Dragon-Duke's
gift and the musical art of the Boy.
The Marquis still clung to the Ruby,
the Casket of Silver, and Bow,
Yet deep in his bosom, with each selfless act,
his charity started to grow.

The Bow had belonged to Roberto
(whom some folk still call "Robin Hood");
Its property was to grant unerring aim when used in the service of Good.

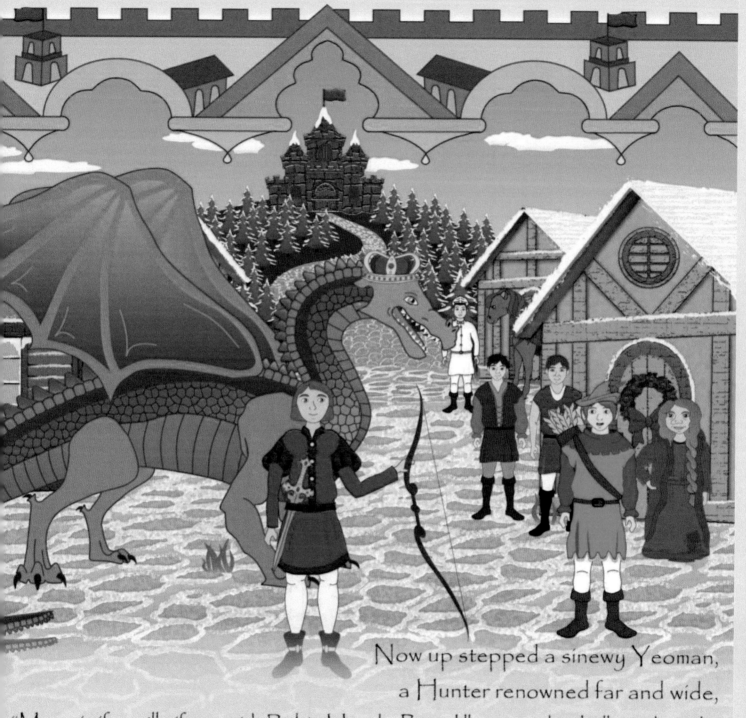

Now up stepped a sinewy Yeoman,
a Hunter renowned far and wide,
"Marquis if you'll gift me with Robin Hood's Bow, I'll use it right gladly, with pride:

"I'll chase the wild deer of the forests, wild boars, and fierce bears of the bosks

"Their meat I'll provide to the Lord's hungry poor, more tasty than mutton or ox

Ah, then who should cheer but the Townsfolk, who'd often felt hunger's sharp bite?
And now in their hearts dawned a love of their lord, who'd formerly earned only spite.

"So next with the Sisters of Mercy, this casket of silver I place,

"For each relic has a miraculous power of comfort and healing and grace."

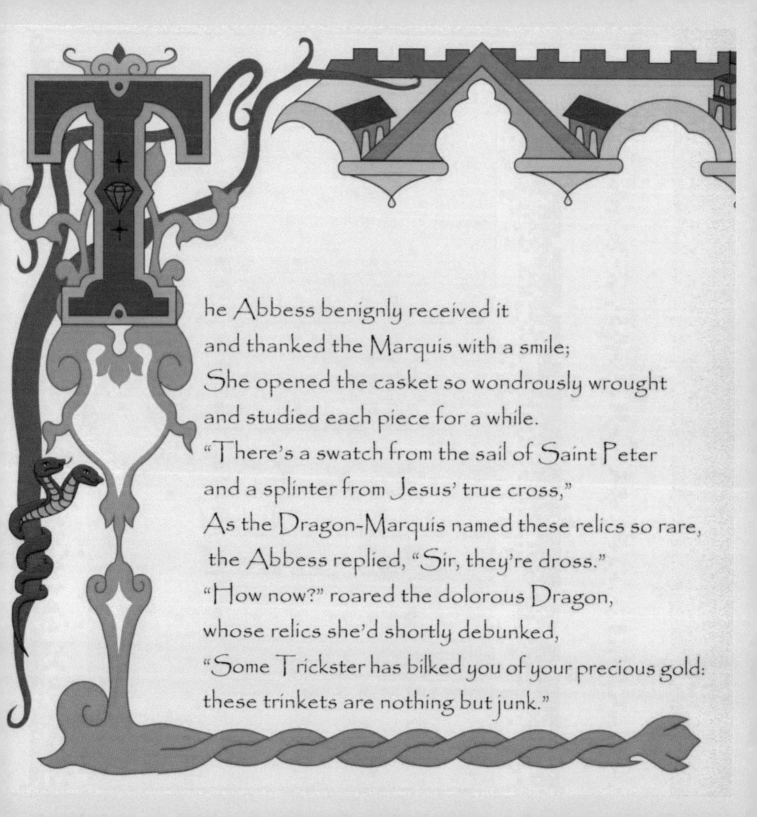

he Abbess benignly received it
and thanked the Marquis with a smile;
She opened the casket so wondrously wrought
and studied each piece for a while.
"There's a swatch from the sail of Saint Peter
and a splinter from Jesus' true cross,"
As the Dragon-Marquis named these relics so rare,
the Abbess replied, "Sir, they're dross."
"How now?" roared the dolorous Dragon,
whose relics she'd shortly debunked,
"Some Trickster has bilked you of your precious gold:
these trinkets are nothing but junk."

"Dear Abbess of Sisters of Mercy," the dolorous Dragon replied,

"I meant this to be my most charitous gift," and great tears of sorrow he cried.

"Your gift yet resides in this casket," the Abbess made haste to assure;

"We'll melt down the Box shaped of Silver so sheen, to coin into pence for the poor."

"Most gracious of Sisters of Mercy, then let it be just as you say:

"We'll smelt down the silver and turn it to coins, for largess on sweet Christmas Day."

So now naught remained but the Ruby, and everyone paused for a space
Until the most beautiful girl in the town stepped forth with a smile on her face.
'Twas Bella, the innkeeper's daughter, whom the Marquis had loved from afar;

He ever had yearned for her sweetness and joy, yet her birth had presented a bar

For she was an innkeeper's daughter, while he was a lofty Marquis;

His pride had constrained him from calling her name, although it was his deepest wish.

But now she confronted the Serpent,
whose head loomed a fathom above;
"Lord Dragon, please grant me your Ruby this day,
to give to my secret true love."
At those words the dolorous Dragon
felt his heart sink within him like lead,
To think that the maiden he'd secretly
loved had chosen another instead.
But now he discovered he loved her
as never he'd known love before,
For though she had riven his heart nigh in twain,
his wellsprings of love swelled up more.
He nodded, unable to tell her
the dazzling Ruby to take;

She took it and rose to the tips of her toes to press a sweet kiss on the Snake.

'Twas then that the Miracle happened, which the legends relate to this day:

The Marquis burst out of his serpentine form and stepped toward the Maiden to say,

"Sweet Bella, I envy the suitor who somehow has wakened your love;

"May the two of you join in a union of bliss, on which Heaven rain grace from above."
She blushed as she smiled at the Marquis, who wore human shape once again;
"My Lord, I will show you the fortunate one, who was ever a Prince among men."

She stepped toward the marveling Marquis and modestly reached for his hand;
She slipped on his finger the Ruby-set ring, saying "Now I think you'll understand."

The Townsfolk erupted in cheering, as no one had e'er cheered before;
"Now see me betrothed to this Maiden in truth, to marry her at the church door!"

The Christmas feast that year was joyous, enriched by the Marquis' largess,
For he married sweet Bella before the church door, their mutual love to profess.
Attending the Mass was Befana, the strega who'd made all come true,

So Reader, beware of your dragonish thoughts –
or else she might come visit you!

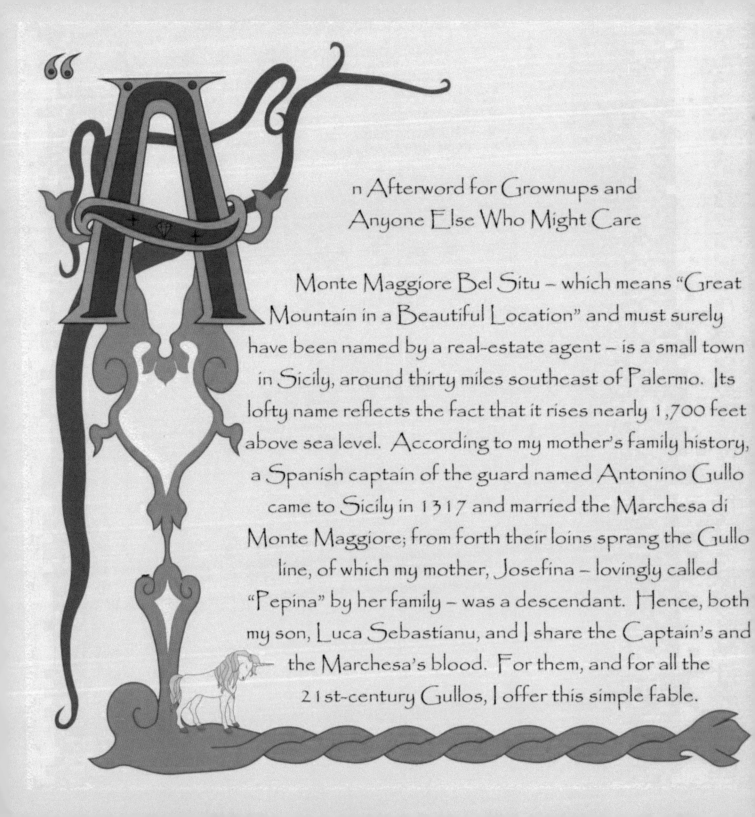

"An Afterword for Grownups and Anyone Else Who Might Care

Monte Maggiore Bel Situ – which means "Great Mountain in a Beautiful Location" and must surely have been named by a real-estate agent – is a small town in Sicily, around thirty miles southeast of Palermo. Its lofty name reflects the fact that it rises nearly 1,700 feet above sea level. According to my mother's family history, a Spanish captain of the guard named Antonino Gullo came to Sicily in 1317 and married the Marchesa di Monte Maggiore; from forth their loins sprang the Gullo line, of which my mother, Josefina – lovingly called "Pepina" by her family – was a descendant. Hence, both my son, Luca Sebastianu, and I share the Captain's and the Marchesa's blood. For them, and for all the 21st-century Gullos, I offer this simple fable.

For those unversed in Sicilian Christmas lore, la Befana is known as "the Christmas Witch (strega)." Although she isn't really a witch, she shares some traits with the American image of witches: she is portrayed as old, shabbily dressed, and somewhat stooped over; and she considers her broom a convenient means of transportation. Simply stated, the legend of la Befana is that she was an old woman of Bethlehem, obsessed with housework; when her neighbors informed her that the infant Jesus had been born in a stable just down the way, she told them she was too busy with her sweeping to stop and visit, but she would catch up with them later. By the time she got around to seeking the Christ Child, the Holy Family had fled to Egypt. Realizing her error, la Befana has searched the world ever since, seeking the newborn Messiah and leaving presents of candy and toys for children everywhere – especially in Italy.

Since I needed a witch for my tale of the Marquis who becomes a dragon (a sort of serpentine Scrooge), la Befana seemed the obvious candidate for the job, and it is no accident that she fits the role splendidly.

Made in the USA
Las Vegas, NV
12 November 2023